THE COLD CAPER!

By Courtney Carbone · Illustrated by Erik Doescher

A Random House PICTUREBACK® Book

Random House New York

Copyright © 2017 DC Comics.
DC SUPER FRIENDS and all related characters and elements
© & ™ DC Comics. DC LOGO: ™ & © DC.
WB SHIELD: ™ & © Warner Bros. Entertainment Inc. (s17)
RHUS 37863

All rights reserved. Published in the United States by Random House Children's Books, a division of Penguin Random House LLC,
1745 Broadway, New York, NY 10019, and in Canada by Penguin Random House Canada Limited, Toronto.
Pictureback, Random House, and the Random House colophon are registered trademarks of Penguin Random House LLC.
randomhousekids.com   ISBN 978-0-399-55844-3 (trade) — ISBN 978-0-399-55845-0 (ebook)
Printed in the United States of America   10 9 8 7 6 5 4 3 2 1

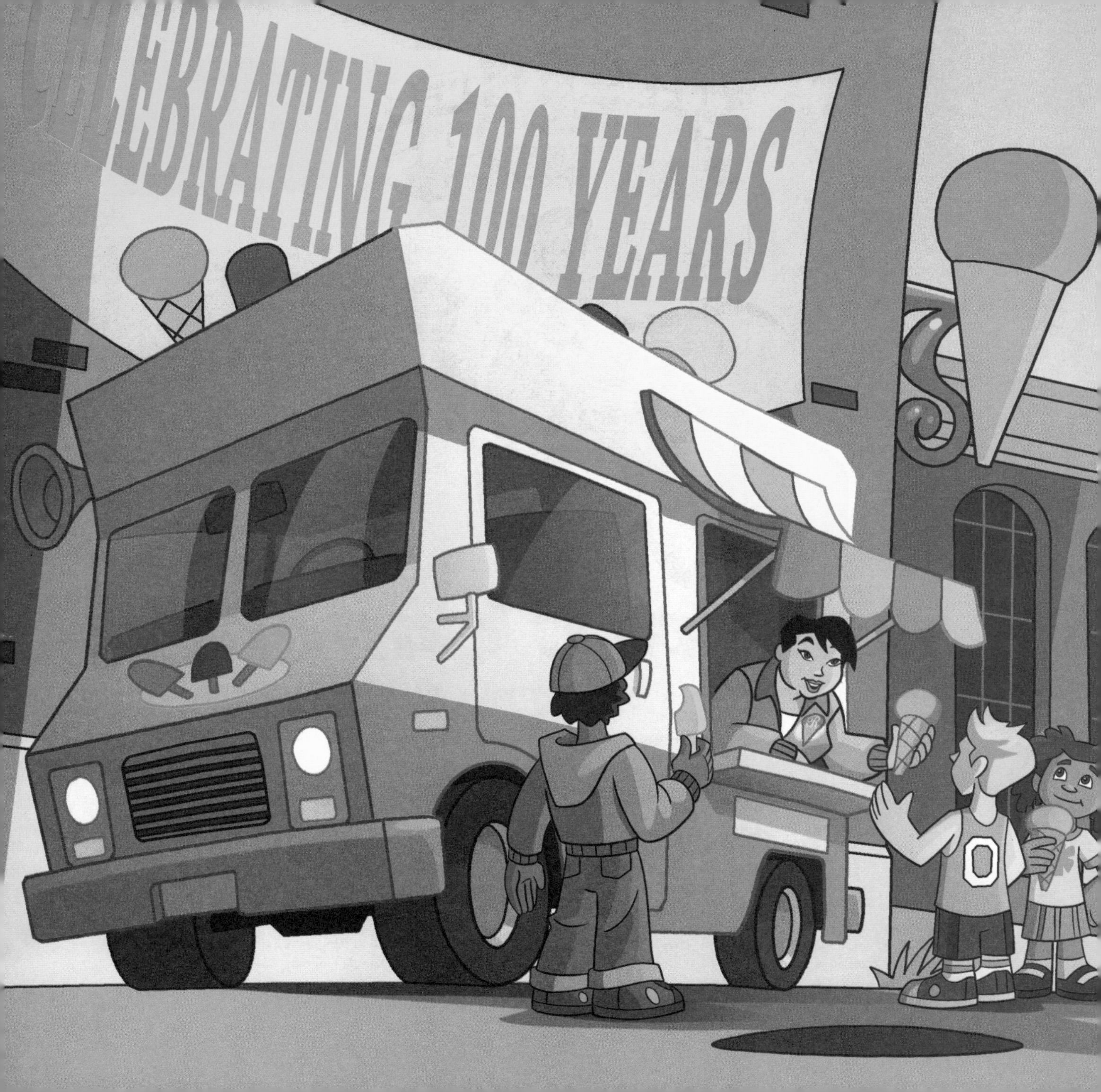
EBRATING 100 YEARS

It was the one hundredth anniversary of the Gotham City Ice Cream Company. To celebrate, the owner, Rose, was giving free ice cream to everyone in the city—as well as one million dollars to a local charity! Everyone was there for the big day, including the super heroes Wonder Woman and Batgirl.

Suddenly, an alarm began to ring. "That's coming from inside the factory," said Wonder Woman. "Someone is stealing the charity money!" cried Rose.

Batgirl and Wonder Woman sprang into action.
"Don't worry, Rose. We'll stop them!"
said Batgirl.

The heroes raced inside and spotted Cheetah and Catwoman!

"What are you two doing here?" Wonder Woman asked, her hand already on her Golden Lasso.

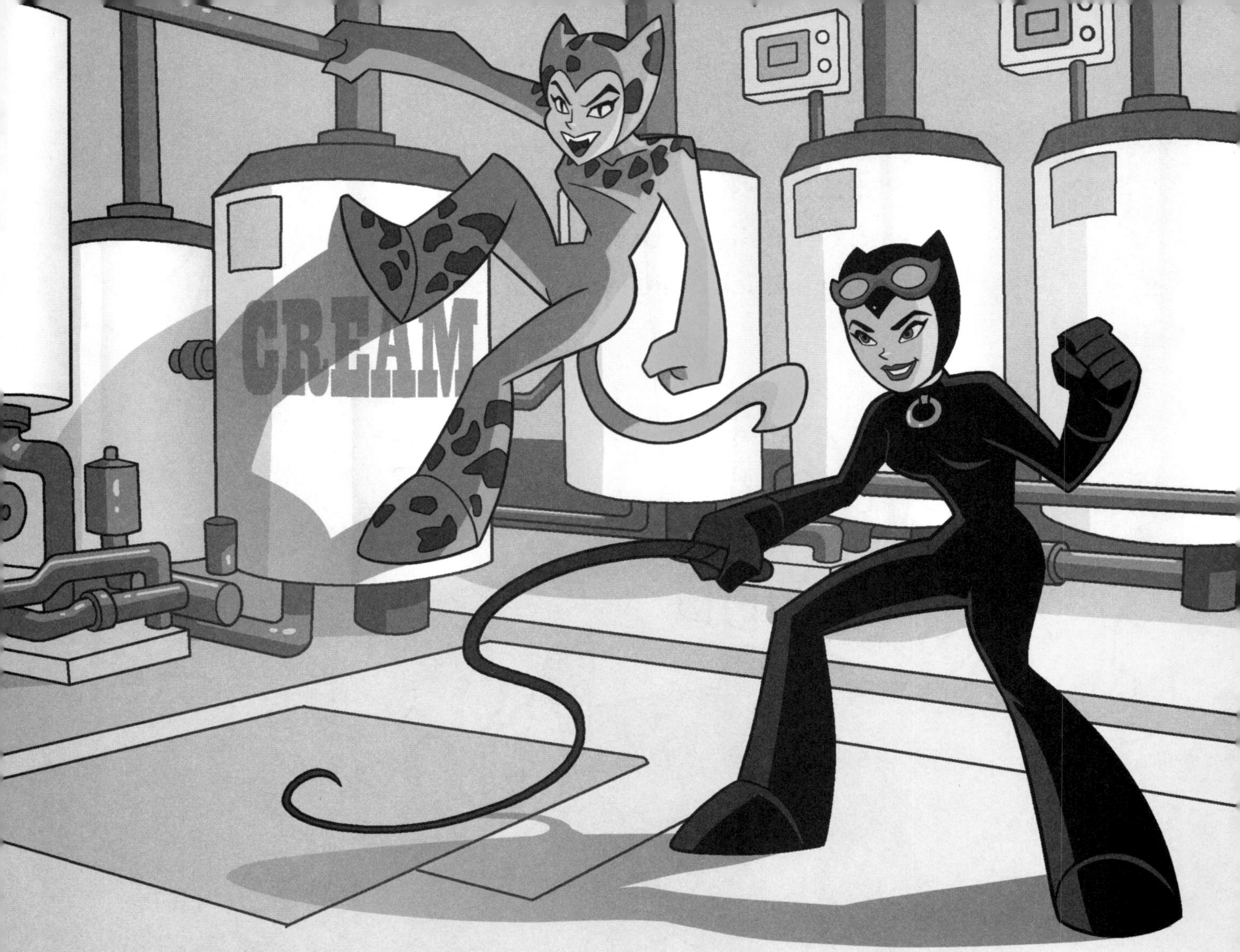
CREAM

“Ice cream always gives us sticky fingers,” Cheetah said, smirking.

“So we thought we’d take ours to go—topped with a nice big sprinkling of cash!” added Catwoman.

The villains sprinted through the factory.
"I've got this!" Batgirl yelled.
"Not if I can help it!" Cheetah replied. She clawed her nails across a huge metal container—releasing a thick white wave of cream!

Batgirl whipped out her Batrope, tossed it over the rafters, and used it to pull herself out of harm's way. Wonder Woman took flight and continued the chase.

Catwoman and Cheetah ducked into another workroom. It was filled with huge mixers churning toppings in enormous vats.

CHOCOLATE CHIPS

PEANUT BUTTER CUPS

TOFFEE

"Hey, Catwoman, let's bring them up to speed!" Cheetah called as Catwoman turned a knob on the control panel. Chocolate chips, peanut butter cups, and toffee pieces flew at the heroes like deadly projectiles.

Wonder Woman jumped in front of Batgirl and used her indestructible bracelets to deflect the high-speed snacks.

Wonder Woman and Batgirl raced after the villains. "Who wants some hot strawberry swirl?" Cheetah asked. She turned a giant handle on a nearby machine, and molten goo poured out. The strawberry syrup oozed toward a group of kids visiting on a class trip.

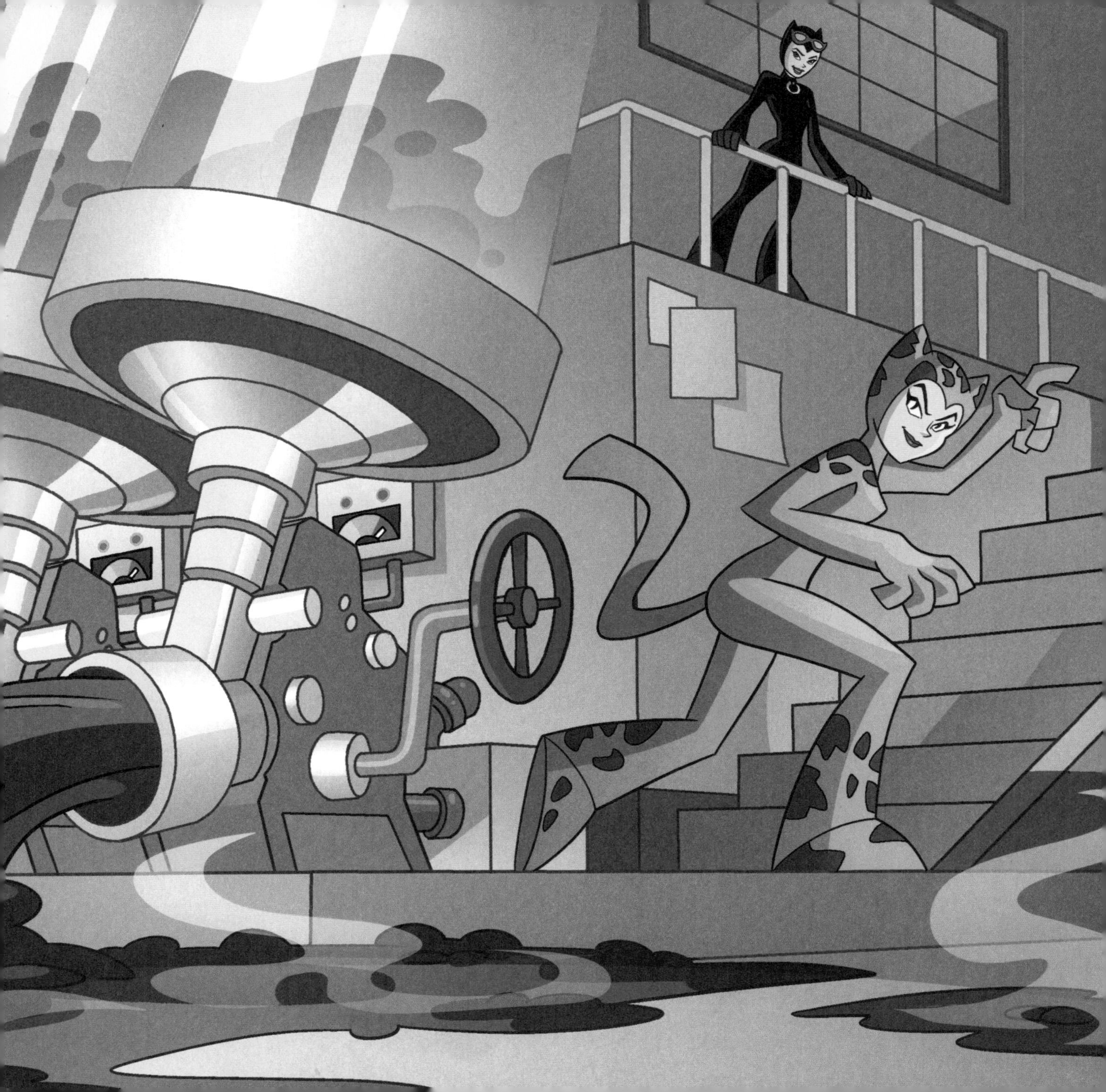

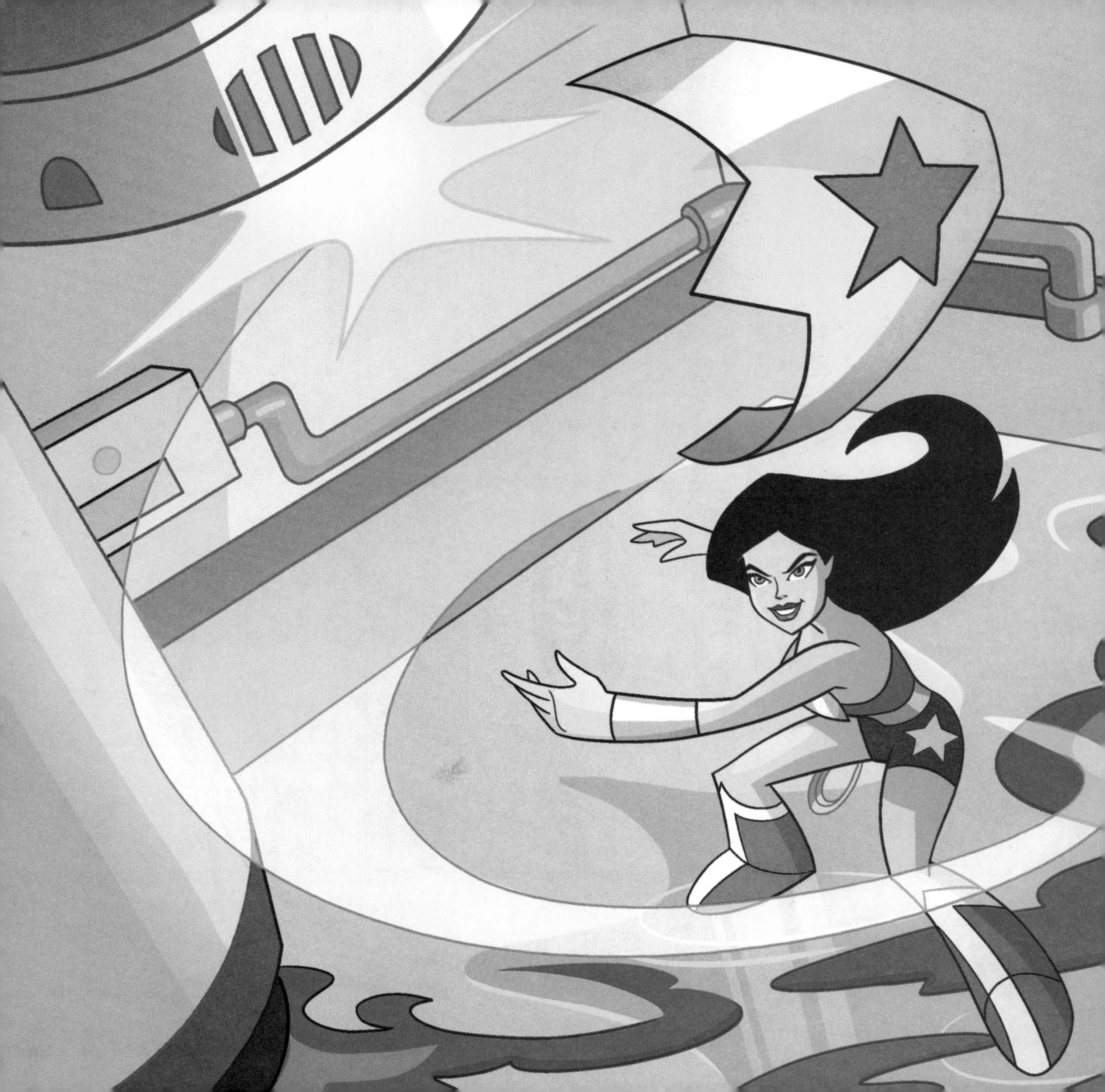

Wonder Woman grabbed her tiara and flung it at a nearby fire alarm. The alarm went off, and water poured from the ceiling sprinklers. The kids cheered as the hot syrup cooled!

Meanwhile, in the office above the factory floor, Catwoman was hard at work trying to break into the safe. The safe had a strong lock, but it was no match for her top-notch burglar skills.

"That's the kind of dough I like," Catwoman giggled
as the heavy steel door swung open.

"Revenge is sweet," agreed Cheetah. The two villains
gathered up bagfuls and clawfuls of the loot.

Then Wonder Woman and Batgirl arrived!
"Hold it right there," ordered Wonder Woman.
"That money is supposed to go to a good cause!"

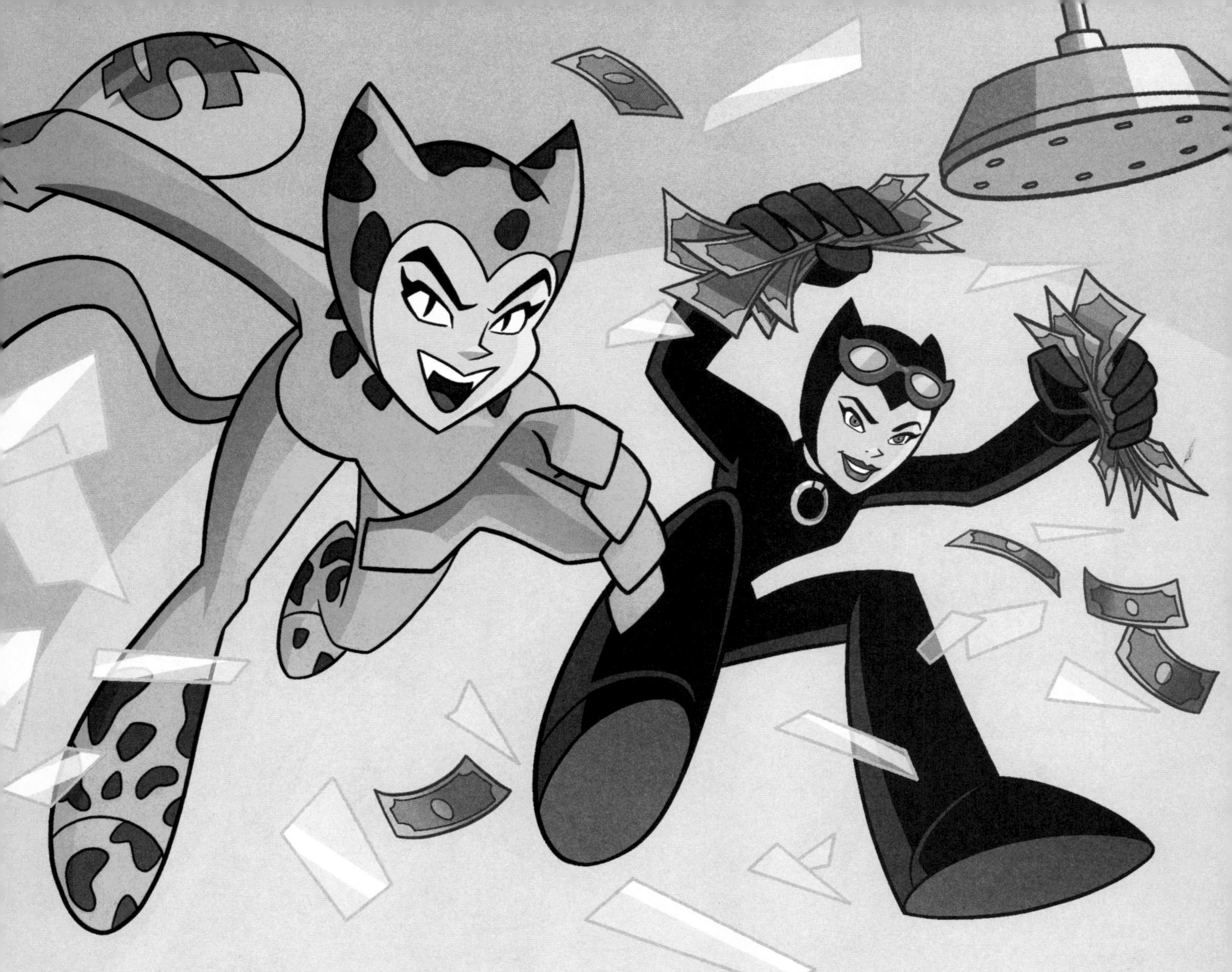

"Who says helping cats isn't a good cause?" Cheetah asked. She and Catwoman smashed through the window and leaped back onto the factory floor.

But the villains had forgotten what a mess they'd made!
The syrup, cream, and candy pieces were everywhere.
Using her lasso, Wonder Woman caught hold of the thieves.
With a great heave, she sent Catwoman and Cheetah sliding
across the slippery mess and into the giant industrial freezer!

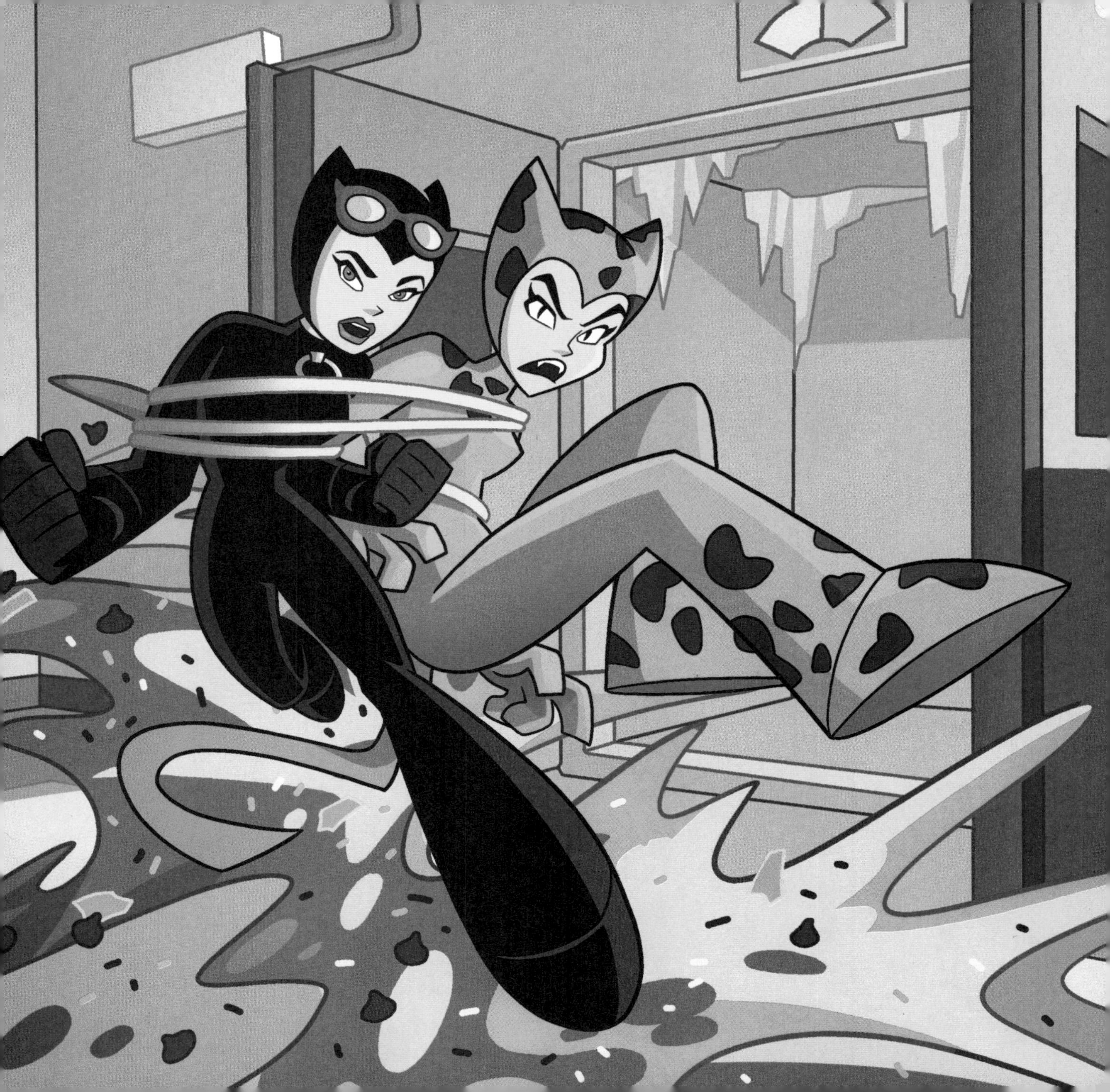

Batgirl closed the freezer door and used a batarang to keep it shut. Catwoman and Cheetah were trapped— and the money was safe!

Just then, Rose arrived on the scene with some police officers. "What do we have here?" she asked, looking at messy Catwoman and Cheetah.

"Looks like you have a new flavor: Cats and Cream!" Batgirl replied.

The police officers took the villains off to jail, and
Rose recovered the money from the freezer.
"Now, that's what I call cold, hard cash!" joked Rose.
"I'm glad everyone got their *just desserts*," added
Wonder Woman.

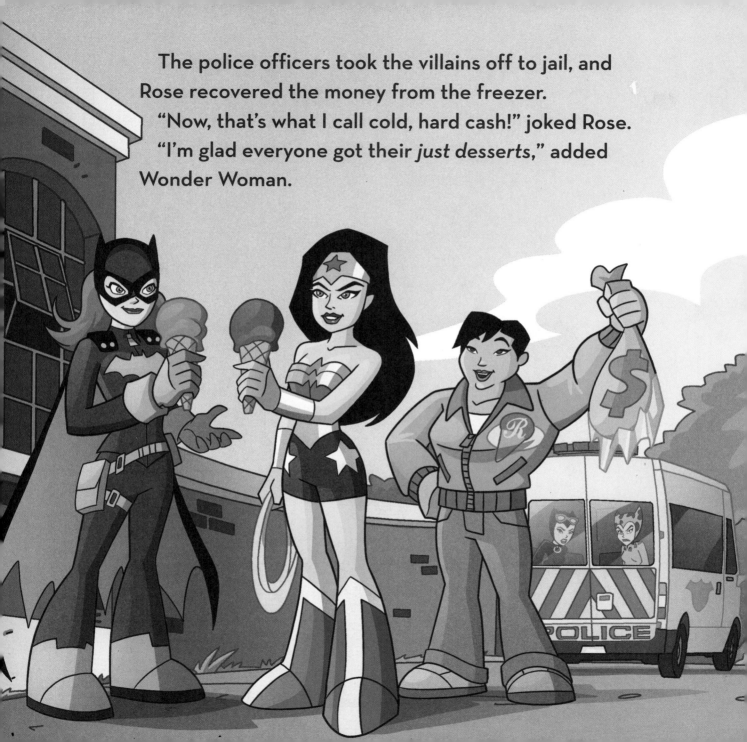